You Can Do It, Sam

Amy Hest

illustrated by Anita Jeram

WALKER BOOKS
AND SUBSIDIARIES
LONDON · BOSTON · SYDNEY · AUCKLAND

It happened one winter morning
on Plum Street ...
and the moon was still up,
making moonbeams and
shadows on Plum Street.

In the little white house, Mrs Bear and Sam were baking cakes. They stirred with big spoons, swirling and tasting batter. They peeked in the oven at two rows of cakes. Golden-brown cakes for their friends on Plum Street!

"Come on, cakes,"
whispered Sam.
"I can't wait,
I can't wait,
I can't wait!"

Mrs Bear and Sam
waited for the cakes.
"Now can we go, Mama?
Now?" said Sam.
"Soon," Mrs Bear said.
"Soon, Sam."

They waited ...
        and waited ...
and then at last
Mrs Bear sniffed the air
with her nose in the air
and said, "I believe
our cakes are ready."

Mrs Bear and Sam counted
the cakes, and there were twelve.
They tucked them in bags, and
there were twelve red bags.

A Tasty Surprise

Outside, snow tumbled
on houses and sprinkled
the trees.

It powdered the garden and Mrs Bear's truck. Sam and his mama climbed up in the truck that was green.

A Tasty Surprise

BEAR 1

They bumped along in the early light.
Just the two of them on Plum Street,
uphill and down, up and down
to the very end of Plum Street.
"Our friends will love my cakes,"
Sam told his mama.
"Of course," Mrs Bear said.

Mrs Bear pulled up close
to the first sleepy house.
"Here we are, Sam. I'll wait here
and YOU take the cake."

"All by myself?" whispered Sam.

"Go, go, go!" Mrs Bear said.

She put her arm around Sam.

"You can do it, Sam."

And off he went.

All by himself in new snow.

All by himself,

waving a red bag and

waving to Mrs Bear.

All by himself,

taking a cake to their friends.

Sam left the red bag
at the door.
(The sign on the bag said:
A TASTY SURPRISE.)

Then he ran back to the truck,
where his mama was waiting.

"I did it!" said Sam.
"Of course," Mrs Bear said.

Mrs Bear and Sam bumped along.

Just the two of them,

uphill and down, up and down.

At each sleepy house, Mrs Bear

stopped the truck.

She put her arm around Sam.

"Here I go!" whispered Sam.
"Go, go, go!" Mrs Bear said.
And off he went, making tracks
in new snow. Waving a red bag and
waving to his mama. Leaving one
tasty cake at each sleepy door.

All by himself ...

until they got home.

(There were TWO cakes left
in TWO red bags!)

"Hmmmm," said Mrs Bear.

"For us?" whispered Sam.

"Of course," Mrs Bear said.

Mrs Bear and Sam held
hands on the path to the
little white house ...

BEAR 1

and the sun was just sunning up
the little white house.
"Hello, house," said Sam, and they
went inside, kicking snow off their boots.

Mrs Bear poured cocoa into cups and
they wriggled their toes in fat socks,
enjoying their cakes with cocoa.
As their bellies filled up,
they took turns telling stories.
Stories about a bear called Sam
who takes cakes (all by himself!)
to his friends ... and how they all
love his cakes so very much!

And that's what happened.
One winter morning on Plum Street.

For Sam. Remember that day,
that walk in deep snow,
on Broadway?
~ A. H.

For Eileen –
Queen of Cakes
~ A. J.

First published 2003 by Walker Books Ltd
87 Vauxhall Walk, London SE11 5HJ

This edition published 2004

4 6 8 10 9 7 5 3

Text © 2003 Amy Hest
Illustrations © 2003 Anita Jeram

The right of Amy Hest and Anita Jeram to be identified as author
and illustrator respectively of this work has been asserted by them in accordance
with the Copyright, Designs and Patents Act 1988

This book has been typeset in Contemporary Brush Bold

Printed in Italy

British Library Cataloguing in Publication Data:
a catalogue record for this book is available from the British Library

ISBN 1-84428-503-0

www.walkerbooks.co.uk